Chapter One

So Antwan say he want to start taking me to church and all our kids. And my stepkids that I get every other weekend now that he married to me and not to her. But it wasn't a Christian church he take me to, see when he got arrested for a dwi he met these Muslim Brotherhood brothers in the jail and they fill his head with a lot of ideas and a lot of religion. But his ideas scare me because I know what Muslim mean at the mosque he take me to, it means he allowed to have multiple wives! I about slapped that brother when I get to the mosque and figure out why he so into it, after I done went through all those years waiting on him to finally marry me. I had to be his baby mama while he was married to a white woman and he kept me on the side.

I already have five kids by him, three girls and two boys. And we aged he and I, and our kids some of them be teens now and we worry they may get in trouble. So he sells me that he will pay they private school tuition, if I will attend mosque and be a good Muslim wife to him. And I want my kids in private school, bad. I want them out of the rough public schools and this Muslim Brotherhood school, it is strict. I agree for the sake of my kids but I beg him please, please no other wives but me. And my husband Antwan, he say, "Don't worry about that now, focus on being a good Muslim wife to me, Shalonda." And I buy the head covering and the clothes and I pray five times a day on a prayer mat. I attend a women's group. And honestly, it wasn't that that sold me. It was seeing my kids change

from the education, we had to send them away
for awhile for a boarding school program and
while they were away they changed them. I
loved who they became, years ahead of they
grade level. And my man, his heart changed.
He stopped making me suck his dick because
that was against our religion. While the kids
were away, he made love to me, really and
truly made love for the first time,
missionary. He didn't make me get up on all
fours and take me from behind doggy style
anymore, the religion said it had to be
missionary. I can't even remember if we had
ever done it missionary but I loved it so much
more this way. He kissed my breasts, and
looked into my eyes. He took me gently, and
I'd never had it that way. And from our
lovemaking, my heart opened up and I realized
it was Allah who changed my man and changed my
kids, maybe he could change me too. The next

day I prayed for real and I felt the presence
of Allah transfigure me. I knew I had to stay
a Muslim. For my kids if I did not appear
devout they would stray. And they were so
happy with the changes in their Daddy. I used
to always be so scared when he would go pick
up my stepkids from his white ex-wife house
that maybe he was getting a piece from her
like he used to do off me.

I was shocked when one day he admitted
it to me. He got down on his knees, and he
apologized. "Shalonda, my queen, I have to
tell you the truth. Remember the night I got
pulled over after dropping off my kids, and I
got that DWI, and went to jail? This religion
saved us, it saved our relationship. If I
hadn't met that brother in the jail that
night, and found Allah, I was on a dark path
that would have led me away from you. I have
to confess, I didn't stop at no bar like I

told you. I had drinks with my ex, and she

sucked me off. I promise that was the one and

only time. But it would have led to more, I

know I would have sinned further against you.

What if I had gotten her pregnant again? You

would have left me, I know you would have.

This is how I know this religion is what we

need. We would've lost each other by now

already. It's already saved this family."

Tears ran down his cheeks.

My man was already circumcised, a

requirement for Muslims, both male and female

at the Mosque we attended. I was terrified of

circumcision. Losing my clitoris? I had

never been a woman who had g spot orgasms

before, so getting my clit cut off would

likely mean I could never orgasm again. That

frightened me, yet I knew African women

culturally received circumcision. I did feel

strangely drawn to it, deep in my bones. And

Antwan began subtly pressuring me to get the procedure done. He gave me books to read, where the women described being able to give themselves release mentally, by imagining the pleasure. But, these were all women who had been circumcised in childhood as was the custom in these other countries. I did not truly believe, if I had been having orgasms with my clitoris to age 40, that circumcision would mean I could mentally have one.

"I really feel upset with you for resisting a full conversion to our religion, for us to be able to seal our marriage properly. Let me be blunt, the way we used to do it, you rarely ever had orgasms with me during sex. You have started having them since we started doing it missionary style, but all those years before, when I hit it from the back your clit didn't get hit. That means all those years you was masturbating, and that is a sin anyway for Muslim women. How would I know you won't continue to masturbate, getting circumcised is the purest way to prove to me you are done with that."

That night, when he climbed on top of me, he shifted the way he laid so that his pubic bone was no longer rubbing across my clitoris the way it had been doing. I kept spreading my legs wider, trying to kind of scoot him more flat on top of me, to get the friction going. I felt hungry for orgasmic release, after all the talk about it. I finally wrapped my legs up and around him, to try to get a grind going that way, but he resisted and whispered, "Lay flat and still for me, honey."

I slowly reached my hand down to finger my clitoris but as he saw my hand touch it he grabbed me by the wrists and pinned my hands back. "Keep your arms up there, don't move.

Hold very, very still," he said, and he smiled down at me. "I want to take you to the Muslim doctor tomorrow for your circumcision," he said. I didn't know what to say. "Feel that tension you have, in your clitoris," he said. "Take some deep, deep breaths, breathe into it. Move the energy up higher, into your spiritual channels." I breathed deeply. I felt anger and I breathed into it. I felt him grow harder. "Now, feel me, imagine you can feel my cock right now. I'm about to cum, let me pleasure, be your pleasure. The orgasm you want to have right now, wish for that to be your man's pleasure instead of your own. Breathe, and stay connected to me. I'm getting close," he said, and I felt the telltale contractions in his large, firm penis. He powerfully contracted a few times, and then squirted with the contractions and moaned very, very loudly before falling down on top of me. As he fell on top of me his pubic bone rubbed against my clitoris which was on fire and sharply erect.

He withdrew his dick out of me nonchalantly, rolled over, and in a few minutes he started to snore. I got up and went into the restroom. I sat down and urinated. I was so aroused still, and reached down to rub one out. I was just getting started, when the door opened and I was caught. My husband looked horrified, and I felt completely ashamed. "Now do you understand how much this is stressing me out?" he asked. I got up off the toilet and followed him to bed. We laid in silence. "I don't think I can handle being married to an uncircumcised, unclean woman, who masturbates, you're not spiritual enough. I want a marriage that's been given over to Allah.

"I'll do it," I said. "Antwan, you know my love for you and this family and our kids means more to me than sex." Besides, I thought, I'm 43 years old now, it's not like I had that many more years left before menopause. "Oh, thank you Shalonda baby," he said. "I didn't know if you really loved me the way Muslim women really love their husbands, or not. When we go to the mosque I see the men with more than one wife, and I think of how strong their love must be for the man if they can set aside all the nastiness, the orgasms, the jealousy, and just work together to support that man."

Oh dear, it sounded like he wanted more than one wife, too. I laid still and did my soul searching. Once I got circumcised there would be no turning back. That night, I got online and I started reading all I could on Muslim female submission. On one message board, a man explained it like this- what we want for ourselves, we should also want for our sisters. If we were truly Godly, if we had a good husband, and another woman needed a husband too, we would want to welcome that woman into the home. Seeing her be loved and cared for would bring us joy, if we had purged ourselves of the sins of jealousy and greed. So the Muslim way could bring a woman much closer to God. I thought of my past with Antwan, how jealous I had been, how competitive, with the other woman he had fallen in love with. I could feel the poison in my heart. What if I had a way to learn to be a better woman?

The next day, Antwan drove me to a Muslim doctor who conducted my circumcision. Female Muslim nurses held my hand lovingly and stared into my eyes. When I awoke from the surgery the gently pressed a cool cloth over

my head and administered my pain medicine.
Was this the kind of love I had been missing
out on all my life? The sisterhood of living
closely and caring with other women, sharing a
life together. Antwan also cared for me so
lovingly after the surgery. It took a month
for me to heal all the way. I could tell
Antwan had been climbing the walls, because he
had taken the no masturbation policy
completely to heart for the month I was out of
commission. And since the faith only allowed
vaginal sex, I wasn't able to help him out.
When the doctor cleared me he was racing the
car home. I felt tingly down there, and
nervous to make love. "Another wife shore
woulda come in handy the past month. With
them not allowing you to beat off or oral you
kinda need a backup anyway like for during
that time of the month." I was silent but I
actually understood this. I had benefited so

much, Antwan used to expect head when it was my time. I did not have good memories of that, feeling crampy and bloated with his balls on my jaws. He had trained me from a young age to deep throat him, and I had actually feared getting older because he had joked about how good it was gonna feel when I could take my dentures out. I remembered the utterly powerless feeling I used to get, when my period would start, and I dreaded the extended face fucking I knew was to come later. He is a well endowed man, my jaws would be sore. For a man who came so quickly with vaginal sex, he loved to take his sweet time with a blowjob, he reveled in the sensation of my tongue and mouth. I knew he was sacrificing sexually for the faith, yes he still got orgasms but, I knew he really missed my blowjobs but I didn't. I felt freed enough by never needing to do that again, that it

justified my lack of orgasm moving forward.
But the question remained, would the trade of
him possibly taking another wife still be
worth it? I had no idea what that life would
be like. Lost in my thoughts I didn't realize
we were home already. He followed behind me
up the stairs and gave my butt a spank.
Through the long, flowing dress and wrap, I
felt so covered, so modest. I used to go to
such lengths to find sexy clothes to wear for
him. This felt so much freer. Who would have
known a hijab was this freeing? I quickly
turned for the bedroom and undressed. I knew
how bad he needed this. Which seemed silly,
he had interrupted my last chance for orgasm
when he caught me masturbating a month prior,
yet I was worried about him because he hadn't
had one in a month?

He smiled and gazed lovingly down on
me. "Thank you for this gift to me. I know

once you learn to channel the energy you will
be the one thanking me." He entered me and I
was so tight from a month without. He made
loud sounds and it was clear his orgasm
started after his first in and out, and it
lasted for three full pumps, it was a long
one. Messy, too, that I had received a
creampie was an understatement.

"Wow, maybe you'll finally get pregnant
again," he said. I froze. I was 43, I didn't
realize he wanted me to have another baby.
That ship had probably sailed at my age. I
explained this to him, the biology and the
lower odds.

"Well, I plan to make more babies, maybe
we should talk about my option for another
wife." He went on to explain that he had
befriended an Indian Muslim family from Kenya
with a 19 year old daughter.

As he went on to describe this I realized he wasn't asking my permission, this had already been planned. He was getting married in a week's time.

Chapter Two

        I hadn't left the bed after we made

love that afternoon, and I didn't come out for

dinner. I heard Antwan out at the dinner

table with our teenage kids, telling them they

were going to attend a wedding in a week, and

all about their new stepmother, and the rules

for welcoming her to the family. He let our

oldest daughter know that her new stepmother

was only a couple years older than she was,

but not to feel strange about it because that

is the Muslim way. My children had some

knowledge of this already, seeing the men at

the mosque with their older first wife and then some younger wives as well.

I cried because hearing him tell our kids, I knew that this was happening. I needed to be strong. I had already decided on this, it was too late to turn back. I prayed to Allah for the strength and to open my heart up to welcome Antwan's new wife, as a sister wife to me. He came in late, and climbed into bed. Here was this person who had broken my heart again and again and I betrayed myself in a way because I rolled over and put my head in his chest and cried. He held me and stroked my hair. In a strange way, my body was becoming aroused as I wondered about logistics, where would she sleep? Whose bed would he sleep in? How could not knowing my own future be arousing me, and how cruel that I could become so aroused, that my poontang was dripping wet for my man, but I could no longer orgasm, so all that sweet honey was there to lubricate me for my man, my arousal still benefited him. I laid back and spread my legs a little, hoping to indicate to him that I was ready for intercourse for a second time. I was behaving like a cat in heat.

"I could go again, it's been so long. But listen, after this, I don't want to make love again all week. I need to save it for my marriage."

"What? Why?" I asked, incredulous that after a month without he wanted to go without again for no reason.

"She's a virgin. I can't last too long, it might hurt her. She's not black, she's Indian, tiny, probably small down there. But they set the wedding date around her cycles, since I'm hoping to conceive right away, so I also want my sperm count high, I'm hoping she gets pregnant right away. Once she

is pregnant I won't sleep with her at all
during the pregnancy, so babe if you can just
bear with me, soon it will only be you and I
together again sexually, for a full year
during her pregnancy, and postpartum and all
that. You'll be my main squeeze as first wife
babe, don't worry," he said, flashing me that
devilish grin that made me melt. He cared
about me, this was just so he could continue
his bloodline and have more children. I could
understand that. It was a big part of our new
religion, being fruitful. If she got pregnant
quickly he might only sleep with her a few
times. I could get through that.

He climbed on top of me and entered me.
This time he lasted longer. In and out, in
and out, and I felt anger for him rise up in
me as he quickened the pace, I didn't want it
to end, in my heart I was so angry but there
was no place to express it. He was making

sounds of pure joy while his big dick roughly
dug me out, not gentle like he had been but, I
understood he had just cum hours earlier it
probably took more friction to get his second
nut, but still, damn, this dude just told me
and my kids he gets ta fuck a nineteen year
old fuckin Indian Princess virgin next week,
and how we all gotta be good and act right fa
her, damn my anger swelled to its peak of fury
as he grunted with his second big nut of the
day. I hadn't even been out tha bed to clean
myself up from before. He didn't hold his
dick in me or look in my eyes after like
earlier, instead he pulled out real fast,
almost rough again even in the pullout and
that's when I knew it wasn't just gettin' more
rubbin ta cum, he was roughin me up. My anger
fell, almost like a release of my own, and I
felt scared.

"You better be real, real good this week, and make sure the kids are good all week. I can't take no stress, no drama, nothing." I felt gaslit. He changed the way our sex was, then told me to be good. When of course I felt mad, over all of it.

"Soften, right now. Soften that look on your face. You have to be a role model, to Aria, my fiance, and to your kids for when they get married. Show them submission by living it, so we can train this new wife right, train our daughters right. Get that hood rat attitude outta here. Get this house fixed up nice, plan a nice wedding dinner and I need a nice breakfast for Aria for next morning. I let you not come out for dinner tonight cause it's your first time with plural marriage and I get it. But I am gonna turn you sweet this week."

He rolled over and went to sleep. I realized I had forced my own hand by agreeing to the circumcision. Without orgasmic release, I had to find another way to relax and fall asleep. And to deal with my anger. I had no choice but to try to find peace. I prayed, and I felt an Angelic presence relaxing my heart. I was going to follow God's path, and trust in God to relax me. The Koran said women were to submit to their husband's and yes many men in the Koran had more than one wife. Obviously God was ok with that, and I was asked to do one thing, to take care of him. I would try following God's will. My husband was, he hadn't asked for oral or anal sex from me, considered unclean and also against God's will since you can't make a baby. He was called to make babies, he came in me twice today. He did his part, if my body wasn't going to cooperate the commandment pretty much admonished him to take on a younger wife and impregnate her. Oh, how I wished I was pregnant but it wasn't even my time of the month, and then in a few days when I ovulated, he said no sex to save it for Aria's cycle. So, soon, maybe next month or maybe the month after, if it was God's will maybe I could fall pregnant too. I remembered a man at the Mosque who had two wives who were both pregnant at once. He looked so proud. Maybe I could be that for Antwan, and be carrying a baby for him at the same time as Aria. This would show his virility, and his service to Allah. It would show I was submitting well to him too. I prayed for that, and drifted off to sleep.

Chapter Three

    I rose early and dressed in a modest house dress. I prepared a breakfast as well as packed my man a lunch. Rather than kiss me on the lips, or hug me, he kissed me on the forehead. "Peace be with you," he said. I prayed and prayed for that as I scrubbed and cleaned. The day passed quickly, and in the bedroom I began to undress for bed.

"Could you leave your dress on for bed?" he asked, coming around behind me to stop me from lifting it over my head. "I don't want to get too stimulated, it's hard going all week without it and seeing you nude, or in a state of undress, I started to get an erection right away. We have to get to Friday night, so each night, sleep in that. Even a nightgown isn't modest enough for when we have to be chaste."

"But we didn't do it for a month, and you let me sleep nude," I said, bewildered. The housedress was to my ankles and thick, it would be very uncomfortable to sleep in it but it was the traditional housewife garb of a Muslim wife, always modest in front of the children and in case of any guests or delivery men, etc. Muslim women didn't dress revealing unless it was in private for the bedroom and the husband.

"This is very different, because I am about to be with a 19 year old. I haven't ever had a virgin, and I haven't had pussy that supple in decades, since you were that age and before I met you. For a male, getting it that young and tight is the stuff of fantasies and it's about to be real. So I am on overdrive right now with my testosterone.

I climbed into bed and he gave me the forehead kiss again. "Good, chaste first wife. Stay like this and you will have so much power in this marriage. I need you to wait on Aria for the first week for a honeymoon but after that you start training her to take over your duties. You will become a house manager, your scrubbing days are going to be over. There are major benefits to a first wife."

I heard him begin snoring. Wow, so this new wife was actually here to serve me, and him, once we got past the week of making her feel special. I was able to make it to Friday, I kept my attitude in check. Then, the kids and I dressed in our best outfits and rode over to her family's home, for the wedding. It was a small, intimate gathering. I noticed Aria's mother looked stressed. She had two younger daughters, each one a year apart. Her husband, Aria's father was a short, tiny Indian man, but his wife, the mother of the bride, was plump. I wondered which one Aria would resemble. The two younger sisters were gorgeous. As Aria walked out to take her place beside my husband, with me on his other side, I finally got to see her. She was the least attractive of the three sisters. I couldn't see much of her figure in her wedding dress, but she looked to be about medium size, kind of an in between. Her face was not very attractive compared to the two sisters who were actually gorgeous. I

felt satisfied that she was sufficiently

homely. I was prettier in the face and

figure, albeit older. She bowed her head in

respect to me. My husband was beaming as he

said his vows. Once they were married, I was

asked to repeat some vows about supporting

their vows as if they were my own, and

treating her needs as my own. I agreed, after

all, that was the point, to work on my own

control issues and selfishness, this was how a

female earned her way to Heaven. For the men

it was different, they were simply to obey the

sexual commands which, were restrictive on sex

acts and position and in marriage only, were

also an instruction to orgasm within a fertile

wife as often as possible to procreate as many

babies as possible. This was how a man got

into Heaven. For a woman, forgoing her own

needs was the key to eternal life (the

circumcision was the ultimate proof of that but it also served to prevent infidelity since multiple wives meant less sex for the woman, having to share her man.)

It struck me that Aria had possibly never had an orgasm before. I thought of the likely painful evening for her tonight, followed possibly by a painful childbirth (Muslim women were encouraged not to use epidurals, the pain was part of how women put their baby first and sacrificed, it was a proving of holiness like the circumcision). Rather than focus on my husband's pleasure from the act, I decided to try and keep my focus on Aria and her suffering.

After a meal with family we got up to bring her home and her younger sisters cried as they said their goodbyes. Her mother took me by the hand and said, "She's a good girl. She has been trained well in this house. I

believe she will do as you say and serve you
well. She is used to getting the belt when
she deserves it." She pointed over to the
wall and I saw a large, black belt hanging up
on full display in the middle of the living
room.

"I'll hang a belt at home so it matches
what she is used to," my husband replied. "I
will seek in everything to please you husband
and first wife. If I fall short I will always
bend over for your belt and accept my whipping
from either of you with thanks for the
correction as I pray Allah will guide you in
perfecting me as your wife," she replied.

Whoa, this girl was taking submission to
a whole new level. She and I walked out
behind my husband as was custom, and I felt
waves of fear, anger, and, sexual arousal as
we drove home, noticing Antwan driving fast
and noticing an erection rising up in his

pants. He led us both into the bedroom and said goodnight to the children. He had set up a second bed for Aria, right in our room, with fresh sheets. He led us both to the bathroom. He had given me instructions to have a "girl talk" with her because Muslim girls were not given sexual instruction for marriage, and the job fell to a first wife, not their mother. He had placed a bottle of lubricant and asked me to lubricate her down there heavily, outside and in, to prepare her for less pain. Even though pain was how a Muslim wife earned her way, he said she had time for that later but that the first time would be pain enough and he thought we should make it easier on her.

I took her into the restroom, and helped her change into the wedding nightgown she had packed, while our husband unloaded the rest of her things and when I peaked out the

door of the bathroom, he was pulling the
covers back on the new Ikea bed he had put
together and made for her in our bedroom. She
and I each had a bed and that took up a lot of
the floor space now. I asked my new sister
wife if she had been told what to expect for
her wedding night and in true religious
fashion she knew nothing other than to submit
to and please her husband. She didn't look
scared but rather excited. I explained to her
that I was going to help prepare her on her
privates because there was some pain for a
first time with in her marital relations and
this lubricant would help her with that pain.
She thanked me for this and I lifted up her
nightgown. Her body was so youthful and
supple and thin as an Indian girl, a new adult
but also a teenager still. She was glowing,
and I caught my own reflection in the mirror.
I looked good but, I looked like a foties

Black woman who had had a lot of kids, she looked, well, gorgeous comparatively. My face looked tense and jealous. I took a deep breath and poured some lubricant on my hand. I pulled her panties down, she was properly circumcised. I was surprised that as I massaged the lubricant in, she was already quite wet. She moaned a little as my finger slipped inside to try to work some lubricant in, that she was very wet already inside.

I heard the bathroom door open. My husband smiled as he saw me pulling her panties up. "No, need," he said, she can come to bed without them. I pulled them down for her and he took each of our hands and led us into the bedroom. I was still wearing my wedding outfit. "I need to change into my nightclothes also," I said. I returned into the bathroom and I noticed I was hurrying as fast as I could, not wanting her alone with our husband any longer than I had to leave her there. Though I had only been in the bathroom for a moment, when I came out he was in her bed with her and kissing her with full tongue, moving his large tongue in and out of her little mouth, which I thought was a lot of kiss for a virgin who had as far as we knew never been kissed. Yet she took his tongue without cringing, fully accepting him with no push back. I froze. I could feel wetness coming out of my circumcised nether regions. I had prepared myself for the jealousy and anger, but not the sexual charge and horniness. Fully turned on and I couldn't even rub one out. But I felt my focus turn to my man, yes, Aria and I were not the orgasms tonight but our husband's orgasm could lead to a new life tonight and that was the point. My mind went to our religion, to the procreation that Allah commanded.

"Just for tonight, there is a ceremony that a first wife gets included to seal the three of us in this marriage. After tonight, whoever I have relations with I will stay in that bed, and you won't ever be in the same bed again together but for tonight, I was told to have you help with this. Come here honey, I promise we won't get weird here, this is very sacred. A ceremony."

I walked over to the bed and sat down. "Ok you sit up against the headboard and spread your legs and then Aria will lay back into your lap. You can hold her hands." She laid back onto me and I took her hands. It was weird, even though my husband said it wouldn't be. It felt like he was copying "The Handmaid's Tale," as it was the same positioning for a ceremony as on the show. He unbuttoned the bodice to her gown, and pulled her tiny little titties out. He licked and

sucked her little nipples and it took her
breath away. The way she started moaning, I
thought she was going to orgasm just from the
nipple stimulation. He already had his shirt
off but now he took his pants and underwear
off and her eyes bugged out when she spotted
his huge erection. I noticed a little precum
was dripping from his head. He leaned up and
kissed me on the forehead again. Then, he
laid on her and started making out with her
again. Then he did something that seemed a
little off color to me. He got a big wad of
saliva and he spit it into her mouth. That
did seem to shock her a little and he closed
her mouth around it and said, "Swallow." I
heard her gulp. Just hearing that word,
swallow, reminded me of all the oral sex I had
given this man. He absolutely required every
drop be swallowed. While he couldn't get his
knob in her mouth he had figured out a way to

make her swallow him. I recalled my very

first date with him, decades ago, and I was

about Aria's age. I was very excited to make

love to him and he had said "Head first,

that's my rule," and laughed. I began sucking

him, thinking he meant just suck it a little

and then he was gonna stick it but no, by head

first he meant I had to finish him and swallow

him. I had tried to stop when I could tell he

was getting close and he had said, "No, no

baby suck it, suck it." So I knew how much

oral sex meant to this man. As I was in my

reverie, feeling my pussy swell, he spit an

even bigger load of spit into her open mouth

and then went down to her little titties again

while she swallowed the mouth full of spittum.

He sucked the nipples just long enough to

rearouse her and he was ready to enter her.

He hiked her nightgown way up and spread her

legs. I gripped her hands to prepare her. He

was able to penetrate her and break her hymen without too much effort, though at some point he couldn't just keep easing it in slowly and had to hunch down and go ahead and pop the cherry to get in. I regretted that I hadn't thought to lay a towel down for the blood spots. She never cried out, and I was glad for that with the kids home.

My husband rocked himself in and out gently and came at his fourth full penetration… he held himself inside her after, holding her hips and staring into her eyes, and then looking up into my eyes with a soft, hazy expression. He withdrew very carefully, probably hoping not to spill out any semen. I got up and went to the restroom to get her her panties, and to change my own panties that were completely soaking wet. I handed her her panties. She was smiling and looked so happy. My husband looked incredibly happy, too. This

was the part where I was supposed to be happy
for them. I shut off the light and I climbed
into my bed. My husband was sleeping just
across from me and I could hear him whispering
sweet nothings into her ear. The lovebirds.
I heard her promising to always love him, obey
him, to give him many children. They fell
asleep and I lay wide awake. I cried softly.
I processed my anger and my rage. I wanted my
man sexually, badly. I imagined his penis now
wet with the drippings of another woman. I
imagined him coming into my bed to make love
to me and I knew I would let him even if he
hadn't showered. Such was polygamy. The
minute you add more than one women suddenly
every pussy in the house is willing and the
answer is always yes, brilliant, why would any
man ever deal with one woman when two or more
made him the king?

I feel asleep late only to be woken by the sounds of their lovemaking again. He got him a morning piece. I would've thought they would move more slowly, surely that puss of hers was real sore, but she was taking him good just hours later. Her tiny little Indian hot pocket must have been fucking magical, because my man just couldn't get enough of her all week. I don't know how I survived their honeymoon. She was wrapping her arms around him as soon as he came home, and his tongue would lick hers in front of my damn kids. She would sit in his lap in the evenings, and one night I had had it, and I asked for a word with him. I told him I didn't think it was right, all their public affection that was more than pg rated at times.

"I'm only going to warn you one time," he said. "You're messing in a world you clearly don't understand. Older second wives disappear all the time when they get jealous and they aren't praying properly for help with that. When she gets pregnant, I'm not going to get to sleep with her, I told you that. To protect the fetus it's Muslim law, but also for better chances of impregnanting ones not pregnant. She and I don't have much time, I probably already got her pregnant. You should give her a pregnancy test tomorrow, she hasn't bled yet. But no matter how many wives I bring home, when I am on my honeymoon I will enjoy myself and if you ever try to hold me back like this again, you'll get the belt in front of the whole family."

I put my head down. "Yes sir, I am sorry sir. It will not happen again." He smiled and walked out. I should have kept my mouth shut because he ramped it up, slipping his fingers down the front of her housedress, in her bra, and I went in my room, got out my prayer mat, and said my evening prayers. He

came into the room and watched me pray,

smiling. When I stood up, he took me into his

arms and held me close. "Tomorrow you start

teaching her to take over your chores and I

warned her of that. Tomorrow, if her

pregnancy test is positive, I'm in your bed

and from now on, she lays and listens while I

make love to my first wife every night. I'm

proud of you."

Aria walked in while he was holding me

in his arms. He released me, walked over to

her, and slid his tongue right in her mouth.

I felt like by the time I got him tomorrow

night, if she was pregnant, he's had so much

pussy for a couple weeks now, it wasn't fair.

I noticed that night he had to pump her a bit

longer than usual to get his rocks off, he was

already getting desensitized. But I was

wrong. When her pregnancy test came back

positive the next day I was thrilled. He
wouldn't get any off her for nearly a year!
And she took to the cleaning chores well, he
was right, I had a woman to do most of my
work, put out babies for him, but as first
wife, my bed came first.

I almost didn't think he would have the
desire for me, and I was surprised when he got
an erection with almost no foreplay. He slid
into me, and I was completely wet for it. "Oh
baby, it's so easy to get in you. She's so
tight I feel like my cock is being squeezed
off. She'll loosen up with each baby but wow,
I feel like I can move all around with you,"
he said. And he made use of that and pounded
me loud and sloppy. I queefed loudly, he was
drawing his hips so high he had thrust air
into me. It didn't put him off. I did hope
for lovemaking like before but I was also glad
to see my pussy still felt good to him. I

looked over and saw Aria in the moonlight, she was watching us, and a tear slid down her cheek. I couldn't imagine her pain, pregnant, clearly in love, and it would be a year until she had any relations with him again. He had even kissed her on the forehead after he heard about her pregnancy test. But he hadn't kissed me at all I realized. He had pawed a bit at what must have looked like my massive bosom and big black nipples and he hadn't seen my breasts in awhile. That had given him an erection and he had entered me quickly. I wondered if he might want to do some of the extended kissing with tongue and even the spitting like he had done constantly with her all week. Funny how her tiny sensitive little nipples weren't much of a lure to him and she could practically cum from that. It made me wonder if he was withholding that on purpose to ensure she didn't get too much pleasure?

But it could just be that her breasts were too small, he loved my big ones. As if reading my mind he sucked my titties and tears welled up in Aria's eyes again. Even though nipple sucking didn't really do it for me, I couldn't resist moaning loudly for effect, she deserved to feel the jealousy I had been tortured with. Watching her watch me got my juices flowing down there again, I had started to dry up. As I got slicker the change in sensation made Antwan cum finally.

Chapter Four

        Aria was emotional from the pregnancy

hormones, but she did her housework dutifully.

Antwan took to kissing her on the forehead now

when he left for work, and then giving me a

long, sexy, sensual kiss. My life was now the

bee's knees. I didn't give a damn that once a

year he got to fuck another woman, when that

woman waited on me hand and foot as first

wife. It was well worth it. I thought my

life was going to be perfect, that was until

my daughter became a legal adult, and I found

out she was to be married to Aria's father. I

realized a bargain had been made, when I saw

Aria's younger sister, now smiling up at my

husband brazenly at the Mosque. I had to

prepare for a wedding both as mother of the

bride, and as a sister wife, for they were

combining the two simple ceremonies on one day.

I tried to speak to Antwan about it. "That man is so old, and small. He's much shorter than our daughter."

"Praise be to Allah you will get to be a grandmother. It's good that he is older. She won't have to provide constant sex the way the younger men want. He is young enough to make babies and that is what matters to our faith."

I didn't dare say a word against his new marriage to Aria's sister, Janae. Janae was certainly the prettier of the two. I wondered about their mother, she had never taken a second wife. At the ceremony her husband could not hide his arousal, I literally saw a tiny little peg of an erection in the Indian man's jeans. My daughter had been inducted into marital submission from the private Black Muslim boarding school she had been to. I knew Aria had gotten the belt a lot in that home and I hoped the wife was not spiteful. She took me aside and said to me, "If you will take care of my girls, I will make sure yours is okay." In that moment I understood the point of this common design. They held my grown daughter Keisha's life in their hands. I had to submit, for my daughter's safety.

Aria looked a bit more troubled since she had had a week of sexual activity, and a baby bump, and knew exactly what pleasures her father would likely be enjoying, based on her own experience now as a wife. She looked over at her mother, and she knew that pain of jealousy in her eyes, too. Her mother would be doing the ceremony tonight. I don't know which one gave her more sadness but certainly tears fell at the nuptials. I think it was a mixed blessing for her, she would get to live out her life with her own sister, but would have to share a husband with her, too.

I had been without any dick for the week per Antwan's honeymoon protocol, and I felt horny. I didn't know what the ceremony would entail with a third wife. I said goodbye to my dear daughter and kept my focus on the point of all these acts tonight, the procreative, the babies for Allah. He had me take Janae in and prepare her with the lubricant. She was just so sexy, gorgeous really. Very shapely for an Indian, with a booty for days. She moaned a little while I lubricated her, and thanked me for it as I had explained the purpose. We got her wedding gown on her, and came out. Aria had been given a chair beside the bed. Antwan explained she would hold one hand and I would be up in the bed and holding the other. We

gave a prayer of blessing for Janae's
fertility and welcomed her. Antwan lifted her
gown off and his eyes lit up. She nestled
between my legs and I figured rather than be
jealous I could enjoy this little porno right
in my own bedroom.

He took Jenae differently. He didn't
do the spitting into her mouth like he had
done to Aria, and I could see Aria's
confusion. At the point where he spent a
very, very long time on her beautiful breasts,
Aria turned her head away and a tear fell.
She grasped her baby bump. He also wasn't as
careful, it was like he had popped one cherry
six months ago and it now didn't phase him the
same to pop another. He kissed her like he
was making love on a beach in the
Mediterranean. She kissed back and it was
like watching two people fall in love, it
hadn't been like that with Aria, they were

more awkward their first time. When he was ready he just pushed himself in her quickly and thrust quickly and came, the intercourse was a lot faster with her than it had been with Aria and I think this spoke to how much more charged they were as a couple.

He shooed me away and spooned her and asked us to get the lights. They damn near didn't leave bed for their honeymoon. With Aria it was like he was breaking us both in. with Janae it was like he lost his senses, of what all was around him. He only saw her, we were periphery. Her first month's pregnancy test was negative, and the second, and the third. He spent nine months fucking just the one woman, other than one time when he took me while she was on her period, and that sucked. He had been feeling Jane's titties and ass in the bed, got a boner he couldn't do anything with since she was on her cycle, and his other wife was pregnant, so he gets into my bed and just spread my legs, no kiss, no foreplay. For a circumcised woman, foreplay from the waist up in all you've got. He had no passion in it, and it took him awhile to finish. That rascal even snuck back over to Janae's bed in the night and I felt pumped and dumped like I used to feel back when he was married to someone else and I was just his baby mama. Back in those days, sometimes there was so much passion between us, and sometimes it had felt like his passion was for his wife and the sex was mechanical. Those were the times my heart broke when he would take off back home and I felt completely used. This night brought all those past feelings back. The difference now was, before I could masturbate at least. Or threaten to cut him off. As a Muslim wife, both of those were now off the table. It was nights like this I felt the

downside of the surrendering I had done.
Things were great with just Aria and I, Janae
had ruined everything. He didn't really seem
all too sad when her pregnancy tests kept
coming back negative, it was like he was
thrilled for another month of pussy with his
favorite girl. Their spell was broken when
Aria's baby daughter was a few months old and
I reminded him she was ovulating and could be
bred again.

He came to her bed that night and I
heard him whisper, "We need to really
concentrate on what we are doing tonight. We
need to make a baby again, Allah willing.
Please open yourself to that completely, and
pray for it while we have our marital
relations."

Aria said "Yes, my king," and grasped
her hands around his neck. She looked so happy
to receive him after nearly a year of forehead

kisses and floor scrubbing. He began kissing her deeply, and entered her with ease now that a natural childbirth had loosened her, just as he predicted. "Are you concentrating, are you praying?" he asked. She said yes. Then he said, "If you don't get pregnant, I'm going to whip you with the belt so I hope that helps you focus. Focus on opening your insides up, be open to your husband's seed. Receive me now fully and completely," he said, as he pumped his hips a lot faster and then groaned, cumming. After he came he remained inside her and bent down for a kiss, spitting a huge mouthful of sputum in her mouth which she swallowed for him dutifully. "I put that load all over your cervix, you better get pregnant off that," he said. He pulled out very, very slowly, so as not to spill out his seed.

And he went back over and climbed in bed with Janae. We were all confused, that Aria

was to get the belt if she wasn't completely
fertile but Janae had had nine negative
pregnancy tests and not a word of a spankin?
Aria did get pregnant again, the girl was a
Fertile Myrtle, because Antwan only copulated
with her that one time. She should have
gotten five or six days of him for the year,
once was a cruelty.

Chapter Five

Aria's first baby was a girl and her second, a boy. Antwan took issue with her parenting, as she was so attached to her firstborn and doting. This was not the Muslim way. In our sect of Black Muslim religion, the little boys were to be completely pampered by all the wives, to prepare them to expect a life of a houseful of doting and dutiful women one day. But not the girls. Girls were to be disciplined and prepared for a live of service and surrender, and taught meekness from a young age. Antwan warned Aria that he would not copulate with her after her recent second birth, once the requisite months had passed and she was eligible, unless she could demonstrate proper discipline of their female little girl. I know she was torn in half by this, she wants relations with her husband and more children, but she struggled to train her toddler to his liking.

    My boys were teenagers and, while they had been taught heavily not to masturbate, I found out my husband was letting them have time with what was called a surrogate, a sexually disgraced Muslim woman who was allowed to stay in the Faith as a teacher of young men, preparing them for their wedding night as a way to avoid being cast out and to keep in housing. My husband had to pay the place that kept her and my suspicion was that my husband had likely tried her out as well, against our faith but not something I could prove and, likely something that went on a lot behind the wives' back. Now that my boys were all 18, they could legally visit the surrogate and, it was hard for me to see them lined up outside the room going in one after another with large erections in their pants. They were under threat that if they were caught masturbating, they would lose the weekly training visits with the surrogate and lose

stature to gain wives, so with only a weekly

sexual release they each took minutes or less

in the room and the woman was escorted in and

out of our home rather quickly.

I became more jealous of the surrogate

than my sister wives, with fears in my mind

that she might be giving my husband oral sex.

My husband would take her in to "get her set

up in the room" and it was all I could do not

to open the door as I felt certain he was

getting head. I wanted to demand to check his

dick after he came out for semen remaining in

the tube, or wetness from saliva but I did not

dare. Something about the idea that Antwan

might be getting blow jobs after all, started

to cause an obsession in my mind and, an

arousal. I started fantasizing about giving

him one again, it had now been years. A chore

I had been glad to get out of, became

transformed in my mind to a power I could
have. I noticed on the Fridays when the
surrogate visited, he didn't sleep with Janae.
I think that is what caused me to obsess, I
saw this surrogate was breaking the spell
Janae had over him and, I wanted that power
over him. One night I had a dream that I gave
Antwan a blow job again, and I had an orgasm
in my sleep! It was delightful. I kept
feeding the fantasy in my mind and it grew and
grew. I did not think of the consequences, or
my faith.

As Aria's ovulation day drew near, she
made a show of giving her daughter a spankin'
and a talkin' to, about the rules for girls,
being quiet, doing whatever Daddy or brothers
say, that God had given men the higher place
and woman's job was to submit. She and Antwan
would take the little girl into her room for a
long stint standing in the corner, and they

held hands. Antwan told Aria she was doing much better now, and when her ovulation test came back positive later in the week, he would give her another baby since he could trust her now to do the right parenting of girls.

Aria was downright giddy the day her ovulation test came back positive, and I let Antwan know. Janae looked jealous but it served her right, Aria and I had suffered terribly for over a year now. My husband had only been with me that once all year and yet I was happy for Aria. She did the brunt of the housework, while pregnant or nursing babies, or both. I encouraged her that Antwan loved her for giving him beautiful children, something I surely couldn't do now at 44. My role was one of house supervisor over she and Janae's chores and the financials and that was about it. I lived in a fantasy world, trying to work up the courage and find my moment to

offer a blow job to Antwan. I had wanted to
wait until after Aria's turn.

He mounted Aria. "Baby number three,
after you give me ten your work is done," he
said. "Allah's will be done," she replied.
He put his mouth over hers and drooled saliva
and then moved his tongue in and out. He
always gave Aria the deepest and most invasive
kisses. Something about her submissive nature
almost invited more invasion from him. He
seemed like he was enjoying himself in her,
probably being the only fertile one he got an
extra charge knowing the sex was procreative.
He had such a different connection with each
of the two sisters.

He surprised all of us by staying all
night in her bed, and Janae and I awoke to a
morning round of lovemaking between them. He
even sucked her little titties and her loud
moaning filled the room. She was

breastfeeding her baby son so Antwan appeared to be nursing from her and enjoying the sweet milk. That night he made love to her again and told her she was a model wife, fertile and obedient, everything a Muslim wife should be. She was beaming the next couple weeks and was thrilled when her third pregnancy was confirmed.

My dirty, sinful thoughts of sucking his cock would not leave my mind, and one night he was in the bathroom brushing his teeth when he asked me to bring him a fresh toothbrush. I came up behind him and put my arms around his waist. "You frisky ain't you? I haven't had you in awhile, I'm sorry. The rules are I'm supposed to stick with Janae until she pregnant," he said sheepishly.

"When will that be?" I asked. "How much longer?"

"Whenever Allah blesses her," he
answered.

"You ain't seem to mind," I replied.

He went and sat down on the toilet and I
decided to make my move. I got down on my
knees in front of him and buried my head in
his lap. He sat up a little and pulled his
boxer briefs down. I needed to feel connected
to him and special so badly. I took his
unerect penis into my mouth and felt him grow
bigger and bigger while I gently licked and
sucked. He stayed quiet and still, but when I
took him deep throat as he had taught me, he
took the sides of my face and we found our
rhythm. He never asked me to stop or tried to
stop me, even though what we were doing was
forbidden. I didn't dare pause, I wanted his
semen down my gullet so badly, I needed to be
the one he came with that night. I could not
bear to hear him cum in Janae's tight little

no baby havin' pocket that he had been glued

to, like a magnet. Just as I had fantasized,

I felt him glued to me now, and decades of

intimacy and routine sprung forth, this man

could never resist my blow jobs, that he had

trained me how to give him exactly as he

liked, when I was Janae's age. I had

something with him that the others didn't

have. He silently squirted his hot liquid

down my throat. He stood up and got the fuck

out of there without a word to me. That night

I could see I had really disrupted things.

Janae was being her usual sultry self but he

knew he couldn't give it to her. His other

wife was pregnant. Whose bed would he climb

into? If he got into mine, they would expect

that meant he and I would have sex but, at his

age he couldn't go again that soon. He got

into bed with Janae and I heard him grow

irritated by her advances. "Chill, I'm tired

tonight," I heard him grumble and I smiled and rolled over and off to dreamland, where my clitoris still existed and I might be gifted with another nocturnal orgasm. I had found the gateway to get around my circumcision. I felt only joy and satisfaction.

Antwan hit the shower the next night when he got home from work and I slid in there with a towel in hand for him and a smile on my face. He looked disturbed. "You sinned, and you caused me to sin. My seed is supposed to be for Janae."

"But, she isn't fertile," I said.

"It felt good but the only way I can do that again would be if I don't cum, I have to save that for her but if you want to fluff me at night I ain't gonna lie, it feels so good. I spoke to another Muslim man to get advice on this and he said if I don't cum, it's only you that's sinned, not me."

That nigga had found a damn loophole.
Hell no, I wasn't going to fluff him for
Janae's pussy, that wasn't the point. I
declined and he countered that I couldn't
attend Mosque anymore with the family because
I was unclean now. And refusing his
arrangement was a second sin, not being in
submission to my husband. This asshole was
blackmailing me that if I didn't fluff him
with my mouth, I couldn't go to church with my
kids. I couldn't let my sons pay the price,
and defeatedly, when he sat on the toilet and
told me to suck him, I got to my knees. It
still turned me on, it was better than not
getting any contact with a man at all. He
kept getting close and telling me to hold on,
hold still, stop, etc. He even called me a
demon, a Jezebel, a sinner, a succubus, every
time he came close he would berate me for it.
I was no longer the circumcised, clean, pure

Madonna in his eyes. I remembered he used to blame me like this when he was cheating on his former wife with me, saying I was hurting his marriage. It was easy for him back then to cheat, yet feel no guilt, by only getting head. And I was so damn lonely back then, when he was married to another woman and popping in on me only random. I remember how when he had had a few visits with the kids after his wedding but hadn't tried to get with me, that I had offered him oral sex and been the one to come onto him, just like this. Maybe he was correct that I was a negative force.

After stopping and resuming four times he told me he was going to get blue balls if he didn't nut soon. He rushed out to the bedroom and by the time I made it in there he was already pulling Janae's nightgown up around her waist and taking her panties down.

She still got affected by my activity, yes he came in her tight little puss but he came after only seconds, no kissing, no lead in. She could tell something was weird. He moaned hard and came for a long time, and the next night in the bathroom he told me the oral sex as foreplay was giving him a lot more pleasure, and a better orgasm.

He held me in his arms. "Since I won't get to spend eternity with you in the afterlife, we have to make the rest of our time together on Earth count." He meant, because of my sexual sins, I would not be going to Heaven with he and his other wives. It bothered me but, I was also very much enjoying our secret world, separate from his other wives. Him saying we needed to make our time together count, meant a lot.

I knew he was probably missing the anal sex he used to subject me to, and I could tell getting oral again had him thinking of other

forbidden activities, because that night while

I gave him his partial blow job, he reached

behind me and fingered my booty hole. I

moaned with pleasure. Other than my nighttime

dream orgasms, it has been so long and I

realized not having a clitoris made anal

stimulation feel extra good. I fantasized

about a rim job he had given me when I was

much younger, before he took me anally for the

first time. Later that night I did some

research online and found out that a large

part of the clitoral complex actually extended

into the anal area, and orgasm through anal

sex was possible for women. Realizing only

the front half of my clitoris had been removed

through circumcision, but that the back half

was up inside me and accessible to my man's

penis, made me hungry for him to take me that

way. Strangely, it was another activity I

used to absolutely dread, that my man loved.

And now, I wanted it but was scared to try,

because it wasn't like he could justify it as

fluffing, religiously, and lay all the sin and

blame onto me. He couldn't take Janae

vaginally with a shitty cock, and that's if he

could avoid even cumming, I knew my husband

and there was no way. If he slid his dick in

my dark, tight ring, he was gonna bust. As I

deep throated him, he sucked his middle finger

to wet it and I trembled knowing where it was

gonna go. Sure enough, he plunged it into my

brown eye, and I moaned, as the electric

thrill of a hint of clitoral stimulation

rippled through my body. I decided to wait on

my man to take the lead anally for now rather

than attempt a seduction. His own soul was at

stake and I didn't want to be blamed by him,

it needed to be his choice.

Seeing my body respond so pleasurably and knowing his cock was being deep throated triggered my man to cum down my throat. I felt my vagina contract with excitement at this unexpected gift and guzzled the cum eagerly, again, what a change, I used to dread his climax and the chore of the swallow he demanded each and every time, and now that my man wasn't supposed to finish with me I worshiped every drop of his nectar.

"Oh no, damn it," he moaned. "You are such a she-devil. I oughtta slap your face but you got me too relaxed to even discipline you," he said, slumping backwards on the toilet, absolutely spent.

"I'm so sorry sir," I said, my head bowed. "I didn't mean to…"

"Right, I know you ain't trying to put your sin on me. Of course you meant to, I sure as hell didn't, I take my commands from

Allah very seriously, I only wish to do my
duty, to spill my seed only inside a fertile
wife as our Scripture commands me. I don't
look at porn no more, I don't masturbate,
nothing. I keep myself clean, but it was you
that defiled yourself just now. That blow job
wasn't for teasin', you purposely milked my
dick and stole my seed from Janae."

"Yes, yes sir, of course I will take
the blame."

I already couldn't go to Mosque and my
kids knew I was unclean. If I had to get the
belt as well that would be hard to take, and I
worried if my man resorted to corporal
punishment I might grow resentful. I wanted
to at least get my pleasure out of this. But
I was more afraid he might end our sessions,
that scared me worse than a spanking. I saw
he was still sincere in his beliefs and

struggling to find his ethics and that made me
love him even more.

"I found out a way I might be able to
get you restored with Allah," he said.

"Really?" I asked.

"Janae is having no luck conceiving. If
I take you to the fertility doctor, as my
wife, Janae can donate eggs to us that I could
fertilize and you could carry. We could have
a lot of babies at once that way, and your
sacrifice would atone to Allah and prove you
are not in the way of a sister wife's
conception."

I froze. Here is where the sacrifice
part came in with this faith. I was only
moments ago fantasizing about getting my ass
reamed by this man and now he was asking me to
carry babies for him and Janae? I couldn't
afford to hesitate here, my soul was on the
line.

"Yes sir of course, anything to be made clean for you again, and for our God."

He reached his arms out and I leapt into his warm embrace, and sobbed. I switched gears back to the Godly wife he needed me to be, surrendered to my man again, and prepared to carry the children he badly wanted for him. I felt the sexual tension that had risen up in me swirling around in my body, and back up into my Spiritual centers, giving me that purer high, yet I caught myself still wondering how long until it might be awakened again down below. To give my womb over to another woman's babies, felt even more intense than my circumcision. I was surrendered and slowly the bliss from that sweet surrender filled me up as my man kissed my face gently, thanking me and blessing me and welcoming me back to our spiritual family and the afterlife.